MYSTERY of the LOST PEARL

Written by Olive Blake

Illustrated by Ed Parker

Troll Associates

MYSTERY of the LOST PEARL

It was one of those days. Nowhere to go.
Nothing to do.

Barney and Barry and Brucie sat on the
steps in front of Barry's house. They sat
with their elbows on their knees. They sat
with their chins in their hands.

Barney turned to Barry. "What do you want to do?" he asked.

"I don't know," said Barry. He turned to Brucie. "What do you want to do?"

"I don't know," said Brucie. He turned, but there was nobody left to ask. So he said, "What a boring day! This day is boring with a capital B!"

Then Barney had a great idea. "I've got a great idea!" he said. "Let's pretend we are private eyes. We can solve mysteries. We can look for clues. We can find things that are lost."

"Anyone can be a private eye," said Barry. "I'm going to be a private nose. I'll sniff out the trouble. I'll smell down the crook!"

"A private nose?" said Brucie. "Who wants to be a private nose? I'm going to be a private ear. I'll listen for clues. I'll hear everything that happens. No one will be able to sneak past me!"

"Then it's settled," said Barney. "We'll call ourselves The Big Three. Private Eye, Ear, and Nose. Our motto will be: See no evil. Hear no evil. Smell no evil."

They shook on it.
"Shake," said Barney.
"Shake," said Barry.
"Shake," said Brucie.

"I want to play, too," said Bubbles.

"It's Bubbles," said Barney.

"Oh, no!" said Barry.

"Go home," said Brucie.

"I am home," said Bubbles. "I live here."

Then Barry remembered. "I just remembered. I have to watch her until my mother gets back." He looked at his little sister. "You know what you are? You are a pest. You are a pest with a capital P."

"I am not a pest!" hollered Bubbles. She stamped her foot. "I am not a pest and I want to play, too!"

"All right. All right," said Barney. "Since you have such a big mouth, you can be a private mouth."

"You mean a *public* mouth!" said Brucie.

Bubbles made a face at Brucie. She licked her lemon lollipop. "I will be a *private* mouth," she said. "I will taste every clue. Even spiders."

"Ugh!" said Barry.

"Yecch!" said Brucie.

"Then it's settled," said Barney. "We'll call ourselves The Big Three plus One. Private Eye, Ear, Nose, *and* Mouth." He looked right at Bubbles. "Our motto will now be: See no evil. Hear no evil. Smell no evil. Taste no evil."

They shook on it again.

"Shake," said Barney.

"Shake," said Barry.

"Shake," said Brucie.

"Shake, shake, shake," said Bubbles.

Just then, Mrs. Piper opened her window. She put two hot pumpkin pies on the sill to cool.

"Good afternoon, Mrs. Piper," said Barney.

"Good afternoon, Mrs. Piper," said Barry, Brucie, and Bubbles.

"There's nothing good about it," said Mrs. Piper. "It's a terrible afternoon. It couldn't be worse. My pearl. My beautiful pearl. I lost it. It fell out of my ring when I wasn't looking. I swept the whole house fourteen times, but it's gone." She held out her finger. The ring was empty. The pearl was gone.

"This sounds like a job for the Big Three plus One," said Barney. "Don't worry, Mrs. Piper. We'll find your pearl. Leave it to us. The Big Three plus One never fails."

Barry stepped forward. He spoke in a deep voice. "Tell me, Mrs. Piper, did you, at any time, leave your house today?"

Bubbles giggled.

"Yes," said Mrs. Piper. "I did."

"Then you could have lost your pearl outside the house," said Barry.

"I could have," said Mrs. Piper. "I could have dropped it on my way to . . . " But at that moment, her phone rang. Mrs. Piper went to answer it. So she never finished saying where she had been that day.

It was a tough case, but The Big Three plus One were ready. That is, Barney was ready. Barry was ready. Brucie was ready. But Bubbles sat daydreaming on the steps.

She was licking her lemon lollipop.

"Come on, Bubbles," said Barney.

"I'm thinking," said Bubbles. "Start without me."

"Where shall we start?" asked Barry.

"Let's split up," said Barney. "I'll keep my eyes open and look for clues." He pointed to Brucie. "You listen." He pointed to Barry. "And you smell."

"Thanks a lot," said Barry.

"Then it's settled," said Barney. He looked at his watch. "It's two o'clock. We'll meet back here in fifteen minutes."

They shook on it. All except Bubbles. She was still thinking.

Barney looked high and low. He looked for clues everywhere. He knew that a private eye has to be smart and look sharp. Aha! A scrap of paper under Mrs. Piper's window. Barney picked it up. There was writing on it. He read:

> flour
> 1 medium pumpkin
> nutmeg
> allspice
> cinnamon
> fig newtons

"It's Mrs. Piper's shopping list!" cried Barney. "She must have gone to the market this morning. That's what she was going to tell us."

Barney followed the trail to Max's
Market. He walked bending over. He looked
everywhere for the pearl.

Then he saw someone else. Someone
else who was bending over. Someone else

who was looking for something. Someone
else who was reaching down and picking
something up.

"Okay," said Barney. "Hand it over!
Give me that pearl!"

"What pearl?" said the somebody else. He straightened up. He was about ten feet tall. He looked down at Barney. "I dropped my dime," he said. "You want to make something out of it?"

Barney gulped. Then he smiled. A friendly smile. "Just a little mistake," he said. "Sorry about that."

At Max's Market, Barney looked under the lettuce. He moved the melons. He looked behind the bananas. He pushed aside the pumpkins.

"Hey!" yelled Max. "What are you doing?"

"A crime may have been committed," said Barney. "Mrs. Piper lost her pearl. I'm looking for it."

"Look somewhere else," yelled Max. "You're making a mess!"

Meanwhile, Barry was sniffing around. He sniffed his way over to a man who sold hot dogs.

"I'm looking for a pearl," he said. "Have you seen one?"

"One?" asked the man.

"Yes," said Barry.

"One hot dog, coming up!" said the man. "Mustard or sauerkraut?"

Barry shook his head. He walked away. He sniffed to the right. He sniffed to the left.

His nose led him to a flower vendor.
"Mrs. Piper lost her pearl," he told the
woman. "Have you seen it?"

The flower vendor held out a bunch of
red roses. "No hablo Ingles," she said.

Barry walked away. He sighed. It was
very hard to be a private nose.

Meanwhile, Brucie was listening for clues. He heard buses going by. He heard cars honking their horns. He heard dogs barking and cats meowing, but he did not hear anything that sounded like Mrs. Piper's pearl.

He listened again. *Coo. Coo. Brrrp.* It sounded like a pigeon. It was a pigeon. The pigeon was strutting down the street. Its sharp, black eyes were looking at something. Something white. Something small. It looked like Mrs. Piper's pearl!

Brucie started to run. The pigeon
stretched out its neck. It picked up the round
white thing. It spread its wings and flew
away.

"Oh, no!" cried Brucie.

Coo. Coo. Coo. Brrrp. Brrrrp.

There were more pigeons. Brucie
looked. Dozens of pearls lay scattered all
over the sidewalk.

"Shoo!" yelled Brucie.

The pigeons flew away. But when Brucie went to look, he found only breadcrumbs. They were small and white. Up close, they did not look like pearls at all.

Brucie looked at his watch. It was two-fifteen. Time to go back and meet the rest of The Big Three plus One.

When he reached his own street, he saw
Barney and Barry. Their hands were empty.
They did not look happy.

Bubbles was still sitting on the steps. It
looked as if she were crying. Mrs. Piper sat

next to her. Probably Bubbles was crying because she had been left alone. And Mrs. Piper had come out to comfort her. What a baby Bubbles was! A great big baby with a capital B!

But when they reached the steps, the boys found Bubbles and Mrs. Piper happy and smiling. Bubbles was having a glass of milk and a big slice of pumpkin pie. And there on Mrs. Piper's finger, round and gleaming, was the lost pearl.

"I found it," said Bubbles. "I tasted the first clue I saw, and there it was."

"*Where* was it?" asked Barney.

"In the pie, silly."

"It must have fallen out when I was mixing the filling," said Mrs. Piper. She poured some more milk. Then she cut a big slice of pie for everyone.

"I would like to propose a toast," she said. "Here's to The Big Three plus One. The best private Eye, Ear, Nose, and Mouth in the whole wide world!"

"Cheers!" shouted Barney.

"Cheers!" shouted Barry.

"Cheers!" shouted Brucie.

"Cheers!" shouted Bubbles.

"Cheers and double cheers!" shouted Mrs. Piper. "And thank you all for finding my pearl."